# Magic Spots

## by Laura Louise Love

Balboa Press books may be ordered through booksellers or by contacting:

Balboa Press
A Division of Hay House
1663 Liberty Drive
Bloomington, IN 47403
www.balboapress.com
1 (877) 407-4847

ISBN: 978-1-4525-2728-4 (sc)
ISBN: 978-1-4525-2729-1 (e)

Printed in the United States of America.

Balboa Press rev. date: 02/02/2015

BALBOA.
PRESS
A DIVISION OF HAY HOUSE

# Praise for Huggi The Bear Magic Spots

"The prospect of what is possible for a child's life with the help of tapping is really exciting, and Laura (and Huggi) make this tool available to children even from a very young age. The playful language and colourful pictures make it an easy and fun introduction for the little kids… and the grownups who love them."

*-Brad Yates — www.TapWithBrad.com — Author of The Wizard's Wish*

# Foreword – Huggi The Bear Magic Spots

*Dr Peta Stapleton*

*Clinical & Health Psychologist | EFT Trainer | Assistant Professor, Bond University, Australia | Author*

It is with absolute pleasure and honour that I am contributing to this world first resource for children by Laura Louise Love. I have come to know Laura well in the last few years and can say with unconditional certainty that she writes from the heart and is filled with a passion to help children cope well with their emotions around the world.

Emotional Freedom Techniques (EFT) have been taking the world by storm for many decades now, and with just cause. The ability to bring up a problem, a negative feeling, thought, behaviour or belief, and turn it off on purpose, is a life long skill to have. It is life changing and life enhancing. What Laura has done in Huggi The Bear is transform the concept of 'psychological acupuncture' or 'tapping' and present it in a way to appeal to children. I doubt there would be many teens out there who didn't relate as well! Huggi The Bear is a magical way of thinking about the acupressure points that can be stimulated with gentle tapping to calm the mind and body, and the rhyming nature of the phrases will entertain the very youngest (and perhaps the very oldest) mind.

As a Clinical and Health Psychologist I specialize in assisting adolescents and adults with issues such as low self-esteem, eating disorders (including obesity), addictions, and other self-harm behaviours. What is often missing in these clients' lives is the ability to let go of a negative thought or feeling. They don't necessarily learn these skills at school, and don't learn them anywhere else. Often we tell children 'build a bridge (to overcome your problem)', or just 'get over it'. But the question they are left with is: HOW?

EFT (Tapping) is a way to actually get over your problems. Right here, right now. And it is easy. Once you learn how to tap, you can apply it anywhere, anytime, and on your own.

I have conducted years of clinical research on EFT for adults and teenagers with a range of clinical problems (from weight loss and food cravings, to clinical depression, to academic fear and perfectionism). We know EFT immediately works and also lasts over time (1 year follow-ups show treatment effects remain). What we are about to embark on are clinical trials investigating teaching EFT to young children, and Laura and Huggi The Bear will be at the forefront of that research. It will be my privilege to be part of Laura's journey as she continues to explore the efficacy of these techniques for children.

So while I truly believe EFT can change lives, help heal the past and carve incredible futures for adults, it is a gift beyond words to offer a child. To know you are truly in charge of your own thoughts, feelings and behaviour and have a way to change them if you find you're not, is a right every child worldwide deserves to have.

*For all the little angels and super heroes out there that love tapping!*

Lots of Love,

*[signature]* x

Over here ...

and under there,
I am your new friend Huggi The
Bear!

My fur is golden and very fuzzy,
I even have a swirly whirly
tummy.

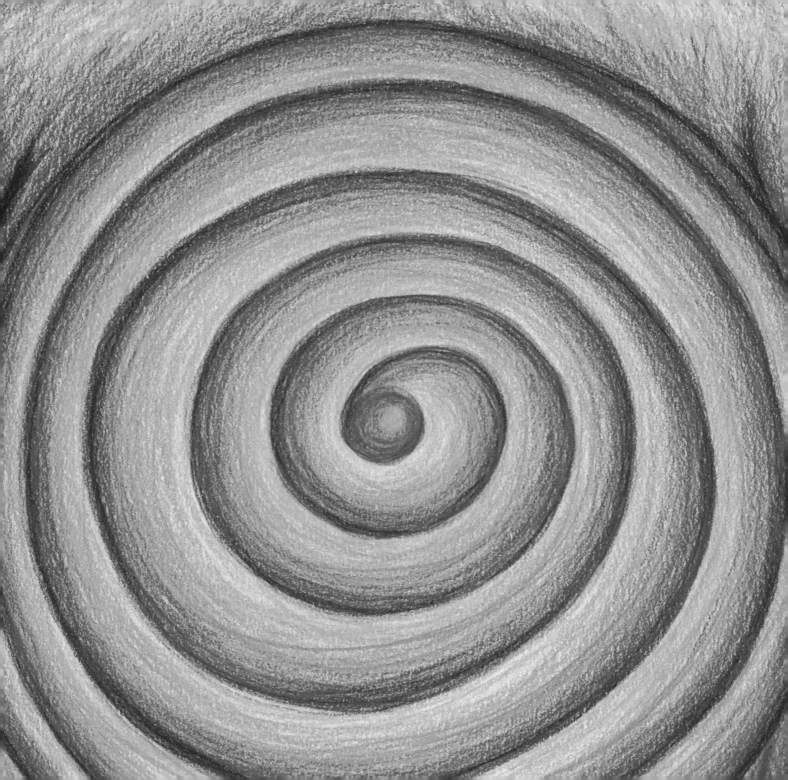

I like butterflies, kisses and
cuddles.
I love rainy days and jumping
in puddles.

I am amazing and I want you to know,
I am a magic bear from head to toe.

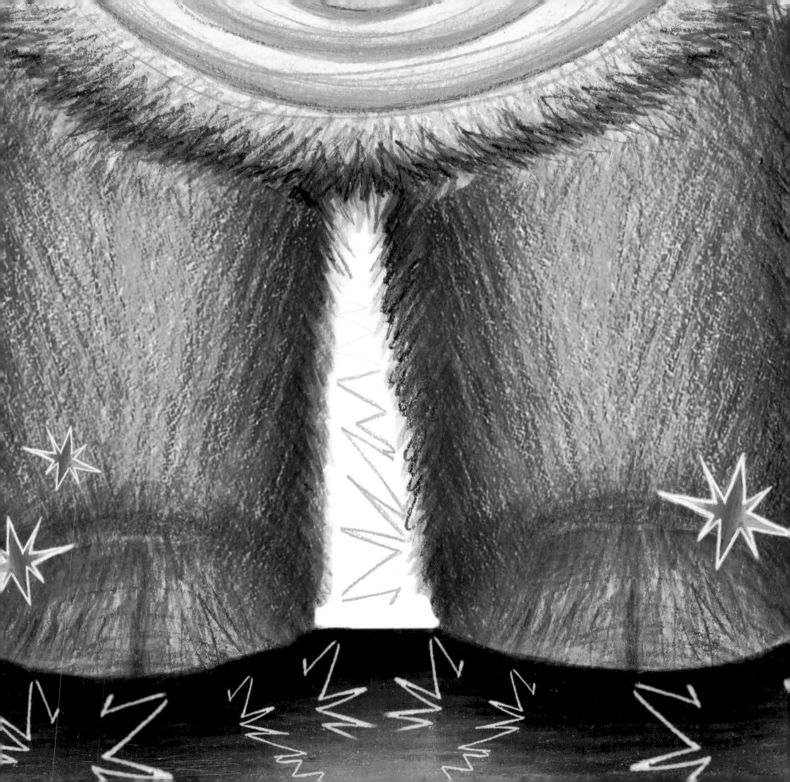

I am from a magical place in the
night sky,
where there are rainbow
sparkles and we can fly!

Zeta is an enchanted place
beyond the stars,
way up high past Jupiter and
Mars.

All the bears in Zeta are happy
just like me.
We bounce around feeling light
and free!

We have these special places we
call them 'Magic Spots'.
Let's tap on them to feel like
laughing lots and lots.

Tap over here ...

and under there,
can you tap like Huggi The
Bear?

Now tap like Tarzan on your chest,
while feeling kind and loved!

Then give yourself a tapping hug!

Let's do them with some nice
warm feelings like... I am safe
and I am happy when I
do my magic tapping.
One more time ... I am kind
and I feel free, I tap myself
and I love being me!

So next time you feel yucky,
tap away those feelings to be
just like Huggi.
I am a lucky bear to have had
our time together. I hope we are
special friends forever and ever!

## For Parents and Teachers

Huggi is a wellness bear who introduces children to a simple version of Emotional Freedom Techniques (EFT), also known as tapping. Tapping is an easy to learn positive coping and self-care strategy. This book called 'Magic Spots' is full of bright, happy illustrations, childlike language and rhyming words, comprised of many from the first 100 words in the national Australian curriculum.

Through Huggi kids can see they have a choice over their thoughts and feelings while learning positive self-talk at a tender age. This book is designed for children that are well adjusted and equally those that are experiencing behavioural difficulties. Tapping is delivered in a simple and effective way by Huggi The Bear and shows children a way to process their emotions. The patterned and repetitive nature of tapping the points stimulate neural systems that reduce stress.

Huggi shows 4 tapping points which are simple, colour coded and called 'Magic Spots' they are;

You can tap, press or rub these while taking deep, relaxing breaths to feel an instant sense of calm. Kids can tap on the pages with Huggi or on themselves. Neural mirroring shows that even if they do not tap, the grown up can tap on themselves while telling the story and therapeutic benefit can still be gained by all! Join Huggi at www.huggithebear.com for loads of free self help resources for children and parents!

## Full Version of Emotional Freedom Techniques for older Children

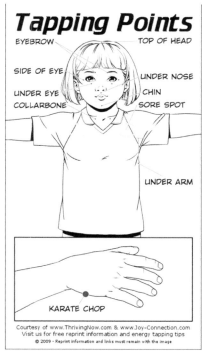

*Image 1. Full sequence of tapping points*

This book introduces children to a simple and shorter version of Emotional Freedom Techniques (EFT) or tapping with the 4 'Magic Spots'. However, the original sequence contains 9 points including the karate chop point on the hand (image 1). These may be relevant to introduce to older children when they become familiar with tapping. The full round of tapping can be something you use as the grown up to process your emotions (for more information see the websites in the Appendix section).

## Tapping with Magic Spots for Anxiety and Stress Reduction

While Huggi has shown children where the 4 points are on the body and the positive statements at the end, an essential part of the tapping process, is acknowledging the negative emotions first. These are what needs to be tapped on prior to the positive tapping rhyme at the end of the book. Children typically tend to store their emotions in their gastro-intestinal region, often reporting things like a yucky, grumbly or aching stomach when something is on their mind. Children may process feelings in many other ways, such as feeling hot in their face, sweaty in their palms or even feeling generally wobbly all over.

Eyebrow: "Yucky"

Under Eyes: "Yucky feelings"

Tarzan Chest: "Lots of yucky feelings"

Tapping Hug: "In my tummy" (or where your child reports)

Eyebrow: "All these yucky feelings"

Under Eyes: "I want to let them go"

Tarzan Chest: "I wish they could go away"

Tapping Hug: "What if they could go away?" (repeat as needed then do tapping rhyme on pg 28)

## About the author

Laura Louise Love (B.A. Psych P.G. Dip. Psych) is a Psychologist in the school education system, with a particular passion for the area of Children's Wellness. She is an author and former commercial model.

Laura is a level 2 EFT practitioner and based on this book her early childhood tapping 4 kids © resilience program is currently undergoing clinical research towards a Doctor of Philosophy.

She created Huggi as a wellness bear that teaches children positive self talk as they are learning to read. Laura is creator and writer of 'Positive Parenting', which are monthly articles freely available online and in school newsletters across Tasmania.

Laura started out her career conducting practical therapy with teens with a disability, children with clinical behavioural problems and those on the Autism Spectrum in early childhood. She is a graduate from Australia's Bond University in the Gold Coast and now lives in Beauty Point, Tasmania.

# Acknowledgements

The original version of EFT for adults was developed by Gary Craig in the 1990's and has been extensively studied since this time. Many researchers, authors and therapists have been credited with further development of EFT as a field. The following people have paved the way for people like myself to adapt the traditional tapping points and present them to young children. They are Ann Adams, Angie Muccillo, Brad Yates, Carol Look, Dawson Church, Dr Peta Stapleton, Natalie Hill, Patricia Carrington, Roger Callahan, as well as the powerhouse brother and sister team Nick and Jessica Ortner. There are also many other figures in the field of EFT. Thank you all for shining a light for me, creating greater awareness of energy psychology and for leading the way for others.

# Appendix

**Laura Louise Love** - *http://www.huggithebear.com/ http://www.lauralouiselove.com/*

**EFT internationally** - *http://www.eftuniverse.com/*

**EFT in Australia** - *http://www.eftdownunder.com/*

**Dr Peta Stapleton** - *http://www.tapintoabetteryou.com/ http://www.petastapleton.com/ http://www.foodcraving.com.au/ http://www.works.bepress.com/petastapleton/*

**Brad Yates** - *http://www.tapwithbrad.com/*

# Disclaimer

Emotional Freedom Techniques (EFT) is still considered experimental in nature although it is gaining in scientific support it is not yet widely accepted as a formally validated scientific technique.

All material and ideas presented in this book are intended to promote awareness of the benefits of learning and applying EFT – however, the general public must take full responsibility for their use of it. This material is for your general knowledge only and is not a substitute for traditional medical attention, counselling, therapy or advice from a qualified health care professional. Neither EFT nor the information here is intended to be used to diagnose, treat, cure or prevent any disease or disorder.

If you experience any unusual symptoms practicing the technique you should seek the advice of a health professional. Although the results of research indicate that many people benefit from the use of EFT with their food cravings, weight loss, anxiety and depression, the responses to the technique are individual. A lack of result, progress or even to know more about administering the technique may require professional assistance.

If you have any concern regarding your health or mental state, it is recommend that you seek out advice or treatment from a qualified, licensed health care professional. The information presented here does not necessarily reflect those of EFT founder, Gary Craig.